What James Said

Liz Rosenberg

ILLUSTRATED BY

Matt Myers

A NEAL PORTER BOOK
ROARING BROOK PRESS
NEW YORK

I'm **never** talking to James again.

We are in a fight.

 James told Aiden,

 who tells everything to Hunter,

 who whispered it to Katie,

 who informed Dante,

 who told it to Emily, Anna, and Declan,

 who let Declan's little sister in on it,

 who told *me*,

that
I think
I am perfect.

I do not think I am perfect.

I have big feet and freckles.

My hair is plain brown.

I am not the best speller

or the best at math.

I am okay at art
but I don't brag about it.
I can't help it if the art
teacher likes me.

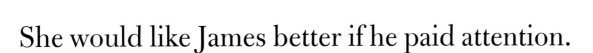

She would like James better if he paid attention.

If he wasn't always cracking jokes

knock knock

or trying to
balance a feather
when he is supposed to be gluing it.

If he wasn't always losing his markers

or saying mean things
behind his best friend's back.

James and I used to be friends, but not anymore.
I am ignoring him.

"What's wrong?" he asked this morning.

I didn't sit next to him on the bus like I always do.

I had to sit between two fifth graders.

"Are you feeling okay?" he asked, while we were hanging up our coats in our cubbies.

I just shrugged.
We have matching
jackets with green
turtles all over and
bright green hoods.

Tomorrow I am
going to wear a
different coat to
school.

I'm not sure he knows we are in a fight.

I sat with my girlfriends at lunch and glared at him across the cafeteria.

He came over and asked, "Do you have a stomachache? Do you want me to walk you to the nurse?"

"No, thank you," I said, and went and threw my lunch into the trash. I wasn't very hungry, then.

Later, James slid
a bag of my favorite
chips onto my desk.

I didn't eat them.

At least not right away.

He drew a funny picture of himself
that almost made me laugh out loud.

Without James to talk to, the school day seemed to last forever.

The clock didn't budge no matter how hard I stared at it.

Finally, we all marched down to the gym
for Art Day. My picture of the beach
was at the front of the room.

"It's perfect," James said.

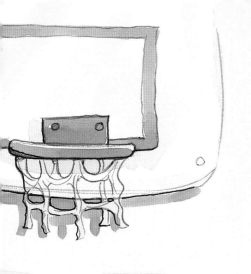

I turned around. "What?" I said.

"I think it's perfect," James said. "That's what I tell everyone."

"Oh," I said. "Thank you."

I didn't hear my name till the art teacher called it out for the third time. She looked mad by the time I got up there. I understood how James felt. She's pretty strict.

Then she handed
me a blue ribbon
and smiled.

Everyone applauded, but James whistled.
He is the best whistler in our grade,
by far.

Somebody took my picture and the
principal shook my hand.

I couldn't wait to sit back down.
I would rather draw all day than stand
up in front of a bunch of people.

James has the beach picture
hanging in his room,
over his fish tank.
He says the Siamese fighting
fish likes the painting.
I let him keep the blue ribbon
that goes with it, too.

The ribbon used to say,
"Best of Show."

Now it says something else instead.

For Neal, best of editors
—L.R.

For Caroline, best drawer of stuff I know
—M.M.

Text copyright © 2015 by Liz Rosenberg

Illustrations copyright © 2015 by Matt Myers

A Neal Porter Book

Published by Roaring Brook Press

Roaring Brook Press is a division of Holtzbrinck Publishing Holdings Limited Partnership

175 Fifth Avenue, New York, New York 10010

The art for this book was created using a cheap ballpoint pen and watercolor.

mackids.com

Library of Congress Cataloging-in-Publication Data

Rosenberg, Liz, author.

   What James said / Liz Rosenberg ; illustrated by Matthew Myers. —

First edition.

     pages cm

  "A Neal Porter Book."

Summary: A little girl ignores her best friend James after she hears

rumors that he has been talking about her, but soon realizes that she

misses his friendship.

   ISBN 978-1-59643-908-5 (hardcover) — ISBN 1-59643-908-4 (hardcover)

1. Best friends—Juvenile fiction. 2. Friendship—Juvenile fiction. 3.

Rumor—Juvenile fiction. [1. Best friends—Fiction. 2.

Friendship—Fiction. 3. Rumor—Fiction.] I. Myers, Matthew, 1960-

illustrator. II. Title.

   PZ7.R71894Wh 2015

   [E]—dc23

                       2014031488

Roaring Brook Press books may be purchased for business or promotional use. For information

on bulk purchases please contact Macmillan Corporate and Premium Sales Department

at (800) 221-7945 x5442 or by email at specialmarkets@macmillan.com.

First edition 2015

Printed in China by Toppan Leefung Printing Ltd., Dongguan City, Guangdong Province

1 3 5 7 9 10 8 6 4 2